Teddy Bear, Teddy Bear

Pictures by Steve Scott

HarperFestival®
A Division of HarperCollins Publishers

Teddy Bear, Teddy Bear,

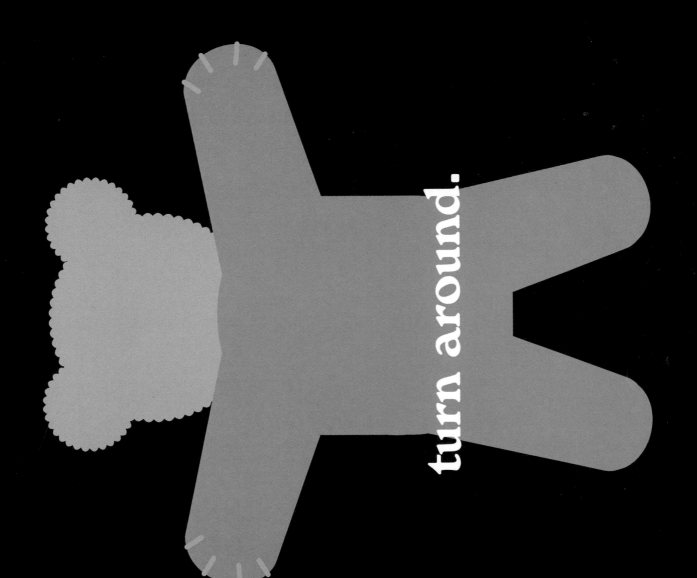

turn around.

Teddy Bear, Teddy Bear,

touch the ground.

Teddy Bear, Teddy Bear,

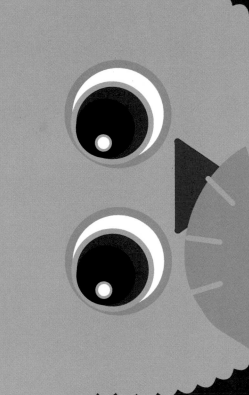

find your nose.

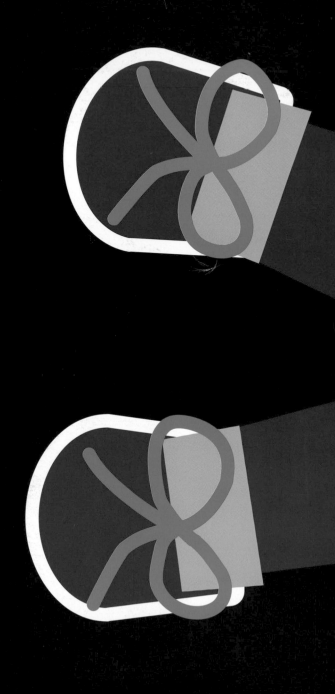

Teddy Bear, Teddy Bear,

dance on your toes.

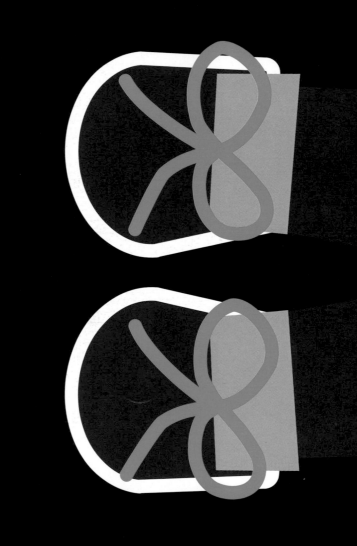

Teddy Bear, Teddy Bear,

jump up now.

Teddy Bear, Teddy Bear,

take a bow.

Teddy Bear, Teddy Bear,

Teddy Bear, Teddy Bear,

say your prayers.

Teddy Bear, Teddy Bear,

turn off the light.

Teddy Bear, Teddy Bear,